GHOST BOY

JAN BURNS

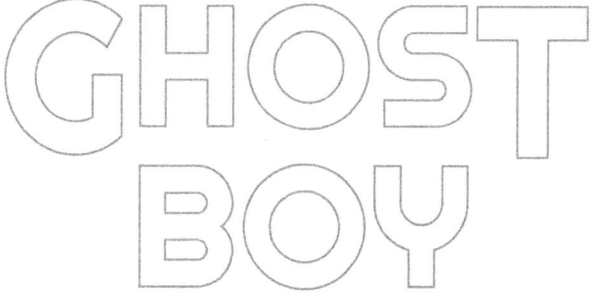

GHOST BOY

A NOVEL

atmosphere press

© 2022 Jan Burns

Published by Atmosphere Press

Cover design by Matthew Fielder

No part of this book may be reproduced without permission from the author except in brief quotations and in reviews. This is a work of fiction, and any resemblance to real places, persons, or events is entirely coincidental.

atmospherepress.com

CHAPTER ONE

Dancing Creek, Texas

I was digging for arrowheads in my grandparents' rock quarry when I saw something that took my breath away.

"Find something, Tyler?" Addy called out.

Addy Robertson and her brother David ran over from where they were also searching.

I bent down and scooped away the rotted weeds from something half-buried in the ground. Then, I wedged my fingers below the edge of the smooth, hard surface to try to pry it free. Surprisingly, the whole thing rolled backward. I was right. It *was* a skull. It looked too big to be from an animal. Plus, there was something underneath. It was a crusty old leather belt with a big initial *B* on the metal buckle.

The quarry sat right behind my grandparents' ranch. Filled with all different sizes and shapes of rocks, it was perfect for us. My friends and I liked to race each other, sliding down the hillsides, exploding clouds of ash-colored dust, and starting noisy landslides of gravel rolling and tumbling to the bottom.

One of us could have slid right on top of this shallow grave and never even have known it. I shivered at the thought.

"You found a skull?" David asked, breaking the silence. He knelt down beside me to look at it closer. "You always find the best stuff."

"That's because I'm always looking around," I told him.

"How did it get here?" Addy asked in a hushed voice.

David knelt down and started digging through the soil around it with his fingers.

"Stop it." Addy reached out and yanked him back by his red t-shirt. "Leave it be."

"I'm gonna go tell your dad, Tyler," David shouted. He turned and dashed toward the ranch house before I could stop him.

"He never could keep a secret," Addy said, frowning.

"Nope," I added, staring after him.

Addy's brother, David, was eight, but sometimes he acted as if he was more than a year younger than Addy and me. Both had dark hair and dark eyes, but that was about all they had in common. More than once, we'd gotten into trouble because of him.

She shoved some stray dark hairs back behind one ear and then said, "I've never seen a real human skull before, if that's what it is. It's creepy. Wonder how long it's been here?"

I stood up and stretched my legs to try to get the feeling back into them after kneeling for so long.

"Don't know," I told her. "Maybe that heavy rainstorm we got a few days ago washed away the dirt that was covering it."

There was still an earthy smell in the air after the rain had soaked the soil. It probably wouldn't last long, though, since the blazing summer heat had returned in full force and was drying things up fast.

Just then, we heard the sound of shoes pounding over the ground. They were coming our way.

When your dad is the town sheriff, you get used to him getting called out at all times of the day and night. But I'd never been there before when he came to investigate something.

Tall with broad shoulders, my dad usually got people's attention right off. He also had a way of narrowing his eyes when he asked questions – like he was looking into your soul.

"We were digging for arrowheads," I told him.

He nodded and then knelt down on the ground to take a closer look at the skull. "It's human alright. Hate to find something like this."

He pulled out a faded blue bandana from his pocket and mopped up the sweat from his forehead and neck. The morning was already hot but not as scorching as it would be in an hour or two.

"By the size of it I think it belongs to a child. I've wondered for years if it would turn up around here someday," he told me.

"Why?" I asked.

Instead of answering me, though, he grabbed the camera that hung over his shoulders and started snapping pictures of it.

"What's next?" I asked after he put his camera down.

"I've called in some people and we're going to see if the rest of the body's here."

David stepped forward. "Can we watch? Please!"

"You can stay if you keep out of the way," Dad said. He shooed us with a wave of his hand toward the edge of the quarry. "Why don't you three watch from under that shade tree over there?"

Two men arrived a few minutes later, carrying picks,

shovels, and other digging tools to the spot where I'd found the skull. Before long, the sounds of shovels and pickaxes smacking the ground echoed through the air, along with the squawk of turkey buzzards who had just swooped down to settle on a nearby tree.

We watched them from under the outstretched branches and shade of an oak tree. The wind picked up, and the oak and pecan trees around us swayed and groaned every time a gust of wind blew through.

"Wonder who died," I said, wiggling the fingers that had touched the skull. They still stung as if I'd gotten shocked with electricity. Whenever I thought about what I'd touched, I felt a strange coldness run through me, despite the heat.

"Looks like they're done," David announced a while later. He nodded toward the men, who were now headed towards us.

My dad led the group, carrying a small box. Even from here, I could see the hard look on his face and knew it wasn't a good time to start asking him questions. That would have to wait.

Deputy Jack Ford pulled up by us just then in a patrol car, noisily throwing a spray of dust and gravel into the air. In his twenties, Jack was every bit as big as my dad.

"Heard you found some stuff," Jack said through his open window. He shook his head. "This is one strange place. Never know what you'll find here."

"Any idea of who it could be?" I asked, walking over to stand beside Jack's car.

"Yep. There's only two people missing from around here that I've heard about. That happened around the time your grandpa was sheriff, Tyler," Jack said. "I heard that case shook up the whole town."

"What happened?" I asked.

"Ask your grandpa about it. He'll tell you," Jack said.

Just then, the men reached us. My dad's shirt clung to his body, soaked with sweat. His eyes looked troubled.

I watched him pass the box to Jack. As he did, his camera, hanging on a strap over one shoulder, rattled and banged against his side as he moved.

"I'm going to turn what you found in when I go and talk with the District Chief in Austin," he said to Jack. Then Dad glanced at me. "I know how you are, Tyler. You're probably itching to find out everything you can about this. But I don't want you getting involved in this case. It's too dangerous. We'll talk about it when I get home. I'll be back in three or four days."

"But," I started to say.

"Nope. Not this time," he said firmly, with a shake of his head. "If I hear you've been out there asking questions, I'll cancel our fishing trip. Understand?"

Next month we'd planned to go to the Colorado River for our annual summer fishing trip. I'd looked forward to it for months.

"Yes, sir," I answered reluctantly.

A hard knot formed in my stomach as I remembered why Dad had already scheduled his trip to see his Chief. He would find out if he was getting a transfer, meaning we'd have to move. I looked down at the ground, not meeting his eyes.

When he turned to leave, I looked back at the spot where I'd found the skull. Suddenly I got the strangest feeling that something big was going to happen, and I'd be right smack in the middle of it.

CHAPTER TWO

Afterward, we went to my grandparents' ranch house. Well, it was really my house now, too, since Dad and I moved in with his parents after my mom died a few years back.

Hundred-year-old oak trees with low spreading branches sat on both sides of the driveway. My grandpa once told me that mountain lions used to prowl this area and climb up onto the lower branches, ready to jump on any prey that had the bad luck to walk underneath them.

"I can't believe you found a skull," David said, slapping me on the back. "We've played around in that quarry a hundred times, and never found anything but a few arrowheads."

"He's right," Addy said with a thoughtful look. "Where did it come from?"

"No idea," I told her. "Hey, are you sure it's okay with your parents if we talk about it?"

Addy shrugged her shoulders. "Before long everyone in Dancing Creek will know about it."

"Okay. Just wanted to check," I told her.

As soon as I opened the front door, I smelled apple and cinnamon, and my mouth started to water. Every year before the county fair, my grandma baked different kinds of cakes and pies, trying out recipes to choose the ones she'd enter into the fair's baking contest.

A few seconds later, eighty pounds of black lab ran up, barking and jumping on my legs.

"Okay, Alanna, settle down," I told her as I rubbed her head the way she liked.

"Tyler, is that you? We're back here in the dining room." My grandpa stood outside the doorway, wearing his usual blue work shirt and jeans. He looked puzzled. "Your dad said you found a skull in the quarry."

"You should have seen the look on his face when he found it," David told him.

"Come in and tell us about it," my grandma said as she waved us into the room. She pushed her glasses up onto her forehead and ran a hand through her curly gray hair. A mountain of bright green county fair raffle tickets lay in front of her on the table. "I've got a pie that just came out of the oven. Anyone want some?"

I did, and Addy and David wanted some, too. Before long, we were eating big pieces of apple pie with a scoop of vanilla ice cream on top.

"Jack said some people went missing, around the time you were sheriff," I told my grandpa, between bites.

His smile faded, and sadness filled his eyes.

"That business about John Casey and his son Ben has haunted me for years," he admitted. "I did everything I could think of to find them, but I never could. It was the kind of case that keeps a law man up at night, staring at the ceiling, asking himself what really happened."

Grandma patted his hand. "You worked night and day on

that case and made yourself sick over it. You did everything you could, which is all anyone can do."

"But I didn't solve the case, did I? Now it looks like Ben's remains have turned up. It's going to start everyone in town thinking about that whole mess again," Grandpa said and sighed deeply.

He took a drink of the strong black coffee he liked and eased himself down into a chair at the table.

"It was the strangest thing in the world," he said. "John Casey used to live right here in this house with his son Ben, who was just about your age, Tyler, when they up and disappeared."

"My age?" Somehow, that made it worse. "What about Ben's mother? What happened to her?"

"Mrs. Casey died from cancer a while before that," Grandma answered.

"So, what happened to Ben and his dad?" David demanded, one hand gripping his cold glass of milk.

"No one knows," my grandma said, setting her coffee cup down on its saucer with a click. "They were here one day and gone the next. It was awful. The news swept through town and scared everyone. We didn't know what to think, or who might disappear next. That kind of thing didn't usually happen in a small town like Dancing Creek."

I stared at her while munching my still-warm apple pie and cold ice cream. Jack *was* right. Strange things *did* happen here. How could people just disappear?

"It wasn't just the disappearance that shook the town. Casey was the foreman of the silver mine that used to be worked here in Dancing Creek," Grandpa said. His eyes hardened. "He disappeared with Ben right after the mine was robbed. I always thought they were kidnapped. But there were others who had all kinds of crazy ideas."

"How was the mine robbed?" David asked, staring at my grandpa. He'd even stopped eating his pie.

"Hush and let them talk," Addy demanded. "I want to find out what happened."

"Well, it wasn't the mine itself that was robbed. It was a shipment of silver ore from the mine that was robbed on its way to be delivered. No trace of it was ever found. It was awful for a small mine to lose a big shipment like that. The whole community felt the shock, because many of the men from town worked there," Grandma said.

"We ordered all the sheriffs around us to be on the alert. But none of us ever found anything. I felt terrible about it – just terrible," Grandpa said, with another big sigh. "John Casey and I were good friends. Right before it happened, I remember thinking he looked like he was worried about something. But he never told me what it was."

Just then, Alanna pushed her cold nose up from under the table and started sniffing.

I knew what that meant. I picked up the last of my piecrust, scooped up some apple filling, and held it under the table.

Alanna ate it up noisily, leaving my fingers wet with dog spit. After wagging her tail so hard it rattled the table leg, she lay back down by my feet.

I wiped my fingers on a napkin, glad I didn't need to use them for eating my pie and sat back in my chair to listen.

My grandmother continued her story. "After the theft, Matthew Roberts, the mine owner, accused Casey. We never believed that. Not for a minute. But when your grandpa went out to question him, John and Ben had disappeared. People said that looked bad, as if that proved John was guilty, and had run away with the silver."

"As best as we could tell, they didn't take anything with

them, either. It was a real mystery," Grandpa said, looking puzzled. "It was like the earth swallowed them up. For months afterwards, I kept thinking they'd come back, and John would explain everything. But, after a year or two went by, I finally had to accept the truth that they weren't ever coming back."

I looked out the back window. Fringed by leafy pecan trees, the quarry looked like a huge bowl carved out of dust and rock. Right now, I felt like I never wanted to go over there again. If I did, I'd remember seeing that skull lying on the ground.

If that skull did belong to Ben, how did it get there? What happened to him so many years ago? I felt that strange coldness creep over me again.

"Your dad said it looked like the dead person was killed years ago and might have been buried in the quarry all this time," Grandpa said. "So that would fit time-wise at least with the disappearance of the Casey's."

"Killed? How do you know it wasn't an accident?" Addy asked, wide-eyed.

Grandpa shook his head. "Tyler's dad said there was a bullet hole in the back of the skull."

CHAPTER THREE

The next morning, when Addy and David rode up on their bikes, I held up a roll of green raffle tickets.

"My grandma asked me to bring these into town, to Mrs. Thorpe at the library," I told them. "While we're there, maybe we can find out more about Ben and his dad. I couldn't get to sleep last night. I kept thinking about them."

When we opened the library's front door a short time later, cool air from the building's four ceiling fans moved around us. The fans' whir filled the quiet, calm space.

The librarian, Mrs. Thorpe, was shelving books when we walked in. She was kind of an in-between age, not young, but not old yet. When she looked up and saw us, she gave us a wide smile.

"My grandmother said to give you these," I said, handing over the big roll of green raffle tickets. "She's working hard on her fair entries."

"Don't you have old newspapers here?" Addy asked. "After what Tyler found, we wanted to try to find out more about

John and Ben Casey."

Mrs. Thorpe nodded, sending her long silver earrings swinging and clicking back and forth. "Everyone's talking about what he found. You know how fast news travels in a small town. Back when all the excitement happened, people didn't know what to think. It just about tore the town up, first with the stolen silver shipment, and then with the Casey's disappearing."

She looked at them thoughtfully. "With this many years gone by, I don't know if we'll ever know what really happened. Now, give me a few minutes to look for those papers."

We took long, slurping drinks from the water fountain while we waited. Then we sat down at a table.

A few minutes later, Mrs. Thorpe carried over an armful of yellowed papers and handed them to us.

"Here's what I found. Looking at these articles brought back a lot of memories. It was pretty exciting when the mine opened. Guess people thought they'd all get rich," she said. "When you're done with them, just leave them on the table. They're not supposed to leave the library."

"These papers smell like stinky old socks," David said, wrinkling his nose.

"If you'd been in that cabinet as long as they had, you'd smell, too," Addy told him with a grin.

"Very funny. Ha. Ha," David said.

We each took a newspaper and looked for articles on the Casey's or the mine.

"These pages look like they're about to fall apart," I said, looking through a paper. The pages crinkled and rustled every time I turned one.

After I'd read for a while, I held up a page. "Here's an article on Matthew Roberts, the mine owner."

"Dang. That's a pretty fancy suit he's wearing," David said.

"I bet he didn't fit in too well here wearing clothes like that."

I had to agree with him there. It was hard to imagine someone all dressed up around here. Most people just wore shirts and jeans.

"Look on this next page – there's a picture of John Casey," David said, leaning over my shoulder.

"He looks like he's a nice guy," Addy added. "That must be his son, Ben, right next to him."

Addy was right. With his shy smile, Casey *did* look like he'd be nice. He had one arm slung loosely around his son's shoulders in a fatherly sort of way. With his short sleeve checked shirt, leather belt with a big "J" on the buckle, jeans, and boots, he also looked like he'd fit in pretty well here.

"Hey, listen to this," I told my friends. "Sheriff Scott confirmed today that John Casey and his eleven-year-old son, Ben, have disappeared from the area. Casey is a suspect in the Dancing Creek Mine theft. His photograph has been sent to surrounding county sheriffs, to be on the lookout for him."

Alongside the article, there was a picture of John Casey standing in front of the mine entrance.

"Did you guys see the news here about the prison break?" Addy asked.

She picked up a paper and began reading aloud. "Around the same time as the stolen silver shipment, two bank robbers escaped from the Leveritt State Prison. They are believed to be headed to this area, since both grew up in Dancing Creek." She pointed to the photos of the men.

When we left the library a few minutes later, I felt like we knew a little more about the Casey's and Matthew Roberts, the mine owner. At least it was a start. That's what my dad always said at the beginning of a case.

The slush place wasn't far away. Addy got strawberry, David got orange, and I got grape. We sat on the front steps, spooning the crushed ice and juice into our mouths.

"These are the best," Addy said. "But I think my mouth is frozen."

David wiped away some orangey juice dripping down his chin with the back of his hand. "It wouldn't be summer without slushies."

He pulled his slingshot out of his back pocket and picked up a stone. Taking aim, he shot at a rotten tree stump nearby. It hit with a loud ping, and a little piece of bark flew off.

"I'll bet you win the slingshot contest this year at the fair," I told him. "What's the prize, anyway?"

"Fifty dollars and a super slingshot," he said, grinning. "I really want to win, so I practice every chance I get. I've got a special place all cleared off on my bookcase where I'm going to keep it."

"You know what dad says about bragging," Addy reminded him.

"Yeah, but when you're good, you're good," David told her. "Tyler, watch my special trick shot."

He turned around twice fast and then aimed. Unfortunately, just then, he tripped and fell flat on his face.

I shook my head and held out a hand to help him off the ground. He was always doing stuff like that.

"You need to practice some more, Mr. Trick Shot," Addy said with a giggle. She squinted into the bright sunlight. "Hey, there's Deputy Jack."

Jack was at the wheel of his pickup truck while a blond-haired guy sat in the passenger seat. Around here, everybody knew everybody, so a new face stood out.

Yet the longer I looked, the more I thought that I'd seen him somewhere before. But where?

After that, we headed home. When we reached the creek about twenty minutes later, I suddenly saw someone way down on the other side of the water. The person was watching us through binoculars. Unfortunately, it was too far away for me to make out what the face looked like.

"Someone's watching us," I whispered, feeling my heart thump faster. "There – by the clump of bushes next to that oak tree."

"Who'd want to spy on us?" Addy asked, shading her eyes and staring out across the rock-strewn creek. "I can't see anyone. You must have super eyesight or something."

"I'll see who it is," David said. Before I could stop him, he tore downstream toward the old stone bridge, his legs pumping hard and his hands cutting through the air as he ran.

I shook my head and ran after him. Some day he was going to get himself, and probably Addy and me, into big trouble.

I could hear Addy running behind me, her shoes pounding the hard ground, like mine. I lowered my head and ran faster. I wanted to see who was watching us, too.

By the time we reached David, he was poking through the thick brushes and brambles. He finally turned towards us, shaking his head. "Whoever it was is gone now."

Addy grabbed his arm. "Why'd you do a crazy thing like that? What if the person had a gun or something?"

David shrugged. "You worry too much. Nothing happened, did it?"

A few minutes later, we got on our bikes and rode back to the ranch.

When we got there, Grandpa came out from the antique shop, which was a little building about fifty feet from the house that he'd remodeled and filled with all kinds of stuff.

"Mrs. Thorpe called from the library," he told us, shading his eyes from the summer sun with his hands. "She sounded pretty upset. She asked if any of you took the papers you were looking at."

"No. We left them on the table," I said. "She told us that the old papers couldn't leave the library."

"She said she couldn't believe any of you would do it, but that she had to ask," he told us.

"What's the matter?" Addy asked, following me up onto the porch.

A puzzled look appeared in his eyes. "Well, when Mrs. Thorpe went to put the papers away, they were gone. Someone had taken them."

CHAPTER FOUR

"What kind of papers were they?" my grandmother asked after we'd all gathered inside the shop.

"They were old ones, from years ago," I told her. "We were trying to find out more about the Casey's and the mine."

Grandma's frowned, and her forehead creased with worry lines. "Tyler, you shouldn't be stirring up old troubles. It could be dangerous."

"What do you mean?" I asked.

"Your dad talked to me before he left for Austin. He thought you might start asking questions about this case. He was worried because there could be someone who would want to keep things buried in the past," she explained. "You have to be careful. After all, the case was never solved."

"Who else was in the library while you were there?" Grandpa asked.

"I didn't really look around," I told him. "Plus, we were mostly way in the back."

"I don't remember seeing anyone, but there were tables

and chairs on the other side of the library, that you can't see from where we were sitting," Addy told him.

"Looks like you've been busy, Grandpa," I said, eager to change the subject. I nodded toward the nearby desk, which had stacks of papers on it. "What are all of those?"

"These are all the records for the antiques I've bought," he told me while scooping up the papers and sticking them in a big black binder. "There's even records of everything I bought from Matthew Roberts' estate sale. I'm going to donate some things to the fair raffle this weekend, so I have to look through these to see what all I have."

"What's an estate sale?" David asked. He picked up an orange from the bowl of fruit my grandparents always kept there, and as he started peeling it, the smell of the orange filled the air.

"Oh, that's just a fancy name for selling the things a person owns after he dies. Roberts died a few weeks after the robbery in a car crash," Grandpa said.

"Give me a few minutes and I'll get a snack ready for you," my grandmother told us.

"I'll give you a hand. That way I'll get first choice at the snacks." Grandpa winked at us. He tucked the binder under one arm and left with my grandmother.

I looked around the shop. *You'd have to be a magician to fit anything else in here*, I thought.

Silver pitchers, cups, and trays, along with sets of china, filled one wall. Ancient-looking books filled a huge bookcase. Another wall was taken up with matching salt and pepper shakers, stitched quilts, fancy glasses, and sparkling jewelry. Everything was crowded together on the shelves, floor, and tabletops, packed so tightly you had to be careful when you moved something – so you wouldn't start a landslide.

Just then, right above my head, a small door at the front of a cuckoo clock suddenly opened, and a little wooden bird shot out, shrieking in a high-pitched tone, "Cuckoo, cuckoo."

Startled, I jumped back and almost knocked over a whole set of pink and white-flowered teacups. Luckily, I stopped myself before I hit the table. Whew!

Addy was frowning at a huge water pitcher that had bright-blue, and mustard-yellow colored flowers painted all over it. "Why would anyone want something like that? I mean, it's not pretty or anything."

"Grandpa says people like to collect things. If they've got one of something, they want a second one to match it. But he says there's another reason people come to antique shops. They try to find valuable stuff. All kinds of finds have turned up that way. Look at these."

I pointed to all the newspaper articles and pictures my grandmother had taped up on the wall. Each showed someone who had found something at an antique store that turned out to be worth thousands of dollars.

"Wow. I didn't know old things could be worth that much money. That's amazing," David said.

"Grandpa once found a diamond in one of the pieces he bought," I told him. "He says that's part of the fun of antiques. You never know what you might find. In some of those newspaper articles on the wall it says people either hide things or just put them away in a drawer or chest, and then forget about them. After they die, other people sell their stuff, not knowing something valuable was inside."

David's eyes lit up. "No kidding?"

"Yeah. Hey, let's take a break and go get our snack."

My grandmother had set out a pitcher of lemonade and some great-smelling apple spice cake in the kitchen for us.

"I think you should enter this in the fair, Mrs. Scott. It's super! Can I have a second piece?" David asked a minute later.

"You haven't even finished eating that one yet," I pointed out with a laugh.

"Yeah, but I know I'm going to want another one," David said, trying to talk even though he already had a mouthful of cake.

"So have you and your dad talked much about maybe having to move?" my grandmother asked me.

I looked down at the red and white checked tablecloth, avoiding her eyes. "He knows I want to stay here."

"He told me he thought if he had a better job in a bigger place - that would give you more security...after your mother died and all," Grandpa said in a soft voice. "You know, anytime you want to talk about it, we're here."

I glanced at him. He was giving me that look that always got to me. I took a deep breath and turned away, afraid I'd get all sad and tell him how much I loved it here and that I never wanted to leave. I only told Alanna things like that.

After finishing the last bites of our cake a few minutes later, we went upstairs. When I entered my room, I saw that my notebook was open on my desk. Walking closer, I could see writing on one of the pages: "Help me. Ben."

If I hadn't been with David all this time, I might have thought it was one of his jokes. I turned to see his reaction to the note.

Any doubts I had about this instantly disappeared when I saw the astonishment on his face. He looked frozen – with his mouth open and his eyes as wide as I'd ever seen them. It looked like he'd even forgotten to breathe!

"David." I reached out and shook his shoulder.

Only then did he come back to life, blinking his eyes several times. "The only Ben I know is the son of John Casey," he finally said.

We all stared at the note lying on the table as if it were a poisonous snake or something.

Addy finally said in a shaky voice, "It can't be real. It can't be."

"Then, who do you think wrote it?" I asked. "Do you think one of my grandparents did?"

"No, of course not," she said.

"Well," David paused and glanced sideways at Addy. "We could talk to Boone."

"Who's that?" I asked.

"Well, he lives in the hills...you know," Addy answered. "We've heard that he's helped other people before with...weird stuff."

I looked back and forth between my two friends. All kinds of rumors and stories had grown up about the hill people over the years. I'd heard that some of them could see into the past or look into the future. They were called *seers*.

Thoughts flooded my brain – about a ghost boy, some seer, and a skull. Then I turned and looked at the note again.

I probably wouldn't have believed it if someone told me they'd gotten a note like this. But, here it was, right in front of me.

What if Ben really was calling out for help?

CHAPTER FIVE

After supper, with David in the lead, we biked to Boone's house. I was glad the road was deserted because I'd told my grandparents I was going over to Addy and David's house, and that was in the opposite direction.

I hated lying to them, but this was an emergency. I needed someone to tell me why in the world a ghost would contact me. How could a ghost even exist?

"I'm not sure about this," Addy said as we rode along. "Do you really believe a ghost wrote that note?"

"I don't know what to think. It's crazy," I told her as I pulled up alongside her. "Who gets a note from a ghost? But I just can't ignore it. No one's ever asked me for help before."

Luckily for us, a light wind had come up that cooled the air and us with it. It was a big change from the blistering heat we'd had lately. As we passed a huge bush of wild red roses, the breeze blew their sweet scent through the air. It was as strong as if someone had sprayed perfume over us.

"What should I say to him?" I asked Addy.

"Just tell him about getting the note," she said.

"He'll probably think I'm crazy or something," I told her, frowning. "He might even laugh at me."

She shook her head. "I don't think so. Wait until you talk to him. You'll see."

"So, have you talked to him before?" I asked, curious about the man she and David told me could help.

"No, but I've lived here all my life, so I've heard about him."

After a while, David shouted, "We're almost there."

We slowly made our way in the fading daylight. Finally, David turned his bike down an old beaten dirt path that twisted and turned to the left into a heavily wooded area.

The ground was so uneven and bumpy that we were forced to get off our bikes and walk the rest of the way. It was hard to see much besides the tangle of overgrown bushes and plants that grew densely around us. Someone long ago must have carved this path through the middle of all the growth.

Every few minutes, I looked around - without knowing exactly what I was looking for - a person, a face - or what.

The night was full of animal sounds. Far off, dogs barked while owls hooted nearby. All around us, insects started their nightly songs of chirps, trills, and buzzes. I loved these familiar sounds of the country.

Beyond the brush, we found a clearing and came upon some wooden shacks at the edge of the hills. A woman with long stringy white hair rocked back and forth in a creaking rocking chair in front of one of them while children ran about noisily kicking a ball around.

Up ahead to the left, we saw an old man using a cane to help himself walk toward us. There were a few people outside the house he'd come from. One of them, a tall, muscular teen, kept looking over at us. It wasn't until the man turned around and nodded to the teen that he turned away.

When he got closer, I saw that the man's bright blue eyes offset his face full of wrinkles.

"That's Boone," David said in a low voice.

The man stopped and spoke. "I wondered if you'd be coming today."

"What do you mean?" David asked. "How could you know we were coming? We didn't even decide to come until this afternoon."

When Boone laughed, his eyes twinkled, softening his tough appearance. "You have a lot to learn. Come on. Let's sit down and talk."

As we followed Boone toward a house, I spotted wind chimes of all shapes and sizes hanging from the surrounding trees. The breeze sent them swaying and playing a tinkling tune as they bounced off each other again and again.

Boone pointed to some lawn chairs shaded by a metal awning, and we sat down.

I pulled Ben's note out of my pocket and handed it to him. "I found this in my room. I don't know how it got there. We think it could be from Ben Casey. Is that possible?"

Boone read the note and then looked up and said, "I heard about what you found in the quarry, and I know all about Ben and his dad disappearing years ago. The news spread through town like the wind."

"After I touched it, my fingers tingled for hours," I told him. "But how could this even be happening?"

"There's no easy way to explain some of the things that happen in this world. They may seem impossible, but they still happen," Boone said. "After they do, you have to figure out what you're going to do about it. That's the big question. What are you going to do?"

I stared at him in astonishment. "You mean you've heard

of something like this happening before?"

He nodded. "People might not want to talk about it, because they don't want to be called crazy. So, they either keep it to themselves, or they come to see someone like me."

"We haven't told anyone else. I didn't think anyone else would believe it," I told him.

"What kind of help do you think he might be talking about?" David asked. "How could he even write the note? Do you think he's real?"

Boone held up his hand. "Whoa. Slow down with the questions."

His eyes narrowed as he studied the note. "Spirits sometimes linger where they died because something remains unfinished for them. So, although Ben's been dead a long time, something has kept him here, at least in a way, even after all these years. Whatever it is, it must be pretty important to him."

"But why does he want *me* to help him?" I leaned forward in my seat, eager to learn the answer to the question I'd asked myself again and again after I found the note. "Why did he come to me?"

"He might have written to you because you found the skull and the belt," Boone said. "Because of that he may feel some kind of connection to you. You said you felt a tingling in your fingers after you touched it?"

I nodded. "Sometimes I still feel it."

He rubbed his chin thoughtfully. "If you're here, though, you must have decided to help him, right?"

"I don't even know how we could help a... spirit," I said. "How would we even find him?"

Boone chuckled. "I don't think you have to worry about that. He'll find you. He's already found you once."

"You mean he'll suddenly show up one day and it will be

like he's alive again?" David asked, wide-eyed.

"No. I don't know if he'll even appear. It takes a powerful amount of energy for a spirit to do that. But, if he *does* appear, what you'll see will only be a kind of a shadow of what he once was," Boone said. "Oh, one last thing. He won't be able to leave the place where he died."

Then he grew serious. "Be careful. Whoever hurt Ben could still be around here. He probably wouldn't want anyone nosing around and asking questions, especially after all these years have passed. There's real danger here."

I stared at him, hearing the clear warning in his voice.

Just then, a strong breeze sent the wind chimes dancing and clanging. As the noise swept over us, I felt like I'd just opened a door and stepped into a totally different world, and I couldn't turn back.

CHAPTER SIX

I woke up late the next morning after spending most of the night waiting for Ben to show up. I'd laid in bed wondering what I would say to him. What do you say to a ghost – or spirit, or whatever he was? I had no idea. But he never came, and I eventually drifted off to sleep.

After I'd dressed and cleaned up, I ran downstairs to the kitchen.

"You feeling alright, Tyler?" my grandmother asked, from where she was sitting at the kitchen table. "Usually you're up pretty early."

"Oh, I'm okay – just had a hard time getting to sleep," I said, looking around to see what was for breakfast. "Something smells good."

"I've got some pancake batter just ready to be used, if you'd like some," she said with a smile. "Grandpa's outside doing chores."

"Sure would. Thanks."

I sat down with a cold glass of orange juice and watched

her pour the pancake batter onto the hot griddle, where it started to sizzle.

As she cooked, I looked out the window and saw the quarry. That made me think of Ben.

I smiled when it struck me that Ben had maybe sat at this same table where I was sitting now. I'd already thought about other ways we were alike. Both of our mothers had died after getting sick. Plus, we were the same age. I bet we would have been friends.

A few minutes later, Grandma sat a big plate of pancakes in front of me, along with the syrup, butter, and some milk. Then, she settled herself back down in her chair.

"There's something I wanted to talk to you about," she said, looking worried. "I thought if you knew a little more about what happened years ago you might understand why I was so worried yesterday, after those papers disappeared."

"You know me, Grandma. I want to be like Dad and Grandpa when I get older. I want to help people. Dad always says you have to ask lots of questions if you want to find answers," I told her while pouring some syrup onto my pancakes.

"I know. I know. But what you don't know is that after the Casey's disappeared, some people thought your grandpa was working with John Casey, in exchange for some of the silver they thought he'd stolen," she said. "Some even came to the house we were living in at the time, thinking we might be hiding the Casey's there."

"But that's crazy," I told her, stunned. "Grandpa would never do something like that. They should have known that."

She shrugged her shoulders. "You and I know that, but at the time people were thinking and saying all kinds of crazy things. You have to understand that people around here were afraid at the time. Things were happening that they didn't understand and didn't like. They also knew that your grandpa and the Casey's were good friends."

Her eyes grew watery, and tears finally spilled down her cheeks. She dabbed at them with her napkin and took a sip of coffee.

Then, she continued her story. "Some people were angry, too. Roberts closed down the mine after the silver shipment was stolen. He said it wasn't making enough money, anyway. When the mine closed, that threw a lot of men around here out of work. They were angry and sometimes took their anger out on innocent people."

She stopped to drink some more of her coffee. I couldn't take my eyes off her. Hearing these things stung as if I'd been slapped.

In a way, it felt like we were going back in time. I could easily picture what it must have been like at the mine when Roberts told the miners he was shutting it down. Like Grandma said, they would have been angry at suddenly losing their jobs. They probably would have wanted a target – someone to blame.

"When your grandpa couldn't solve the case, he took it hard, and eventually resigned. It would have broken a lesser man. But he stayed strong and worked the quarry until he retired," she finished.

I looked away from her and rubbed at my eyes. I wish I had a rock that I could throw or something.

"So, it was hard when you started bringing it all up again," she said. "Your grandfather is a proud man. He never said much, but the whole incident hurt him deeply. That was the only case he couldn't solve."

"It must have been awful," I told her. "I didn't mean to cause any trouble with those papers. But, after what I found, I wanted to learn more. It was like I'd become part of Grandpa's case, in a way. Do you understand?"

"Oh, Tyler," she said, reaching out to put her hand on mine. "You know your dad wouldn't want you to do that, don't you? What do you think he'd say?"

I didn't answer her. There wasn't any need to do that. We both knew very well what dad would say or what he'd do. I'd probably be sent to my room forever. Plus, he'd cancel our fishing trip, where it was just him and me alone, without him always being busy with work.

"I want you to stop asking questions," she told me. "Don't do anything that might be dangerous. Just leave everything be."

I hoped my face didn't let on how her words made me feel, like a balloon that someone popped, so all the air ran out.

"Be careful," she said. With that, she got up and walked out of the room.

After that, I ate five of my grandmother's big pecan pancakes with maple syrup, breaking my old record of four. Then I went out to sit on the shady front porch so my stomach could settle down after its major workout.

I was angry, too. I had the best grandpa ever. How could people who knew him think those awful things about him? It was just crazy.

I watched a cardinal race from tree to tree, its bright red color contrasting with the leafy green branches. A minute later, I heard a loud knocking and saw a redheaded woodpecker with a black and white spotted chest pecking on a nearby tree.

I pulled a slingshot out of an old basket on the porch and picked up some small rocks from the yard. Aiming at the tops of nearby fence posts - *Pop. Pop. Pop.* I hit them all right in their centers.

I wasn't as good as David, but I wasn't half-bad, either.

Just then, Alanna came over from where she was sunning herself on the walk and sat down right next to me. I absent-mindedly rubbed her head.

"I've got a lot to think about, Alanna," I told her.

She turned her head and looked up at me with her big brown eyes, making me feel she knew what I was saying and how I felt.

"How could Ben and his dad disappear, without anyone knowing anything about it?" I asked her in a low voice.

I hated lying to my dad and grandparents about what I planned to do. But some things are so important you have to do them. You just have to. At least that's what I told myself.

Just then, I saw a paper fluttering in the breeze on the far right of the front porch. It was held down by a rock. I went over to see what it was. When I unfolded it, the words in black ink seemed to scream out at me: **Stop asking questions or you'll be sorry!**

CHAPTER SEVEN

"Wow!" David exclaimed after reading the threatening note. "Who do you think wrote it?"

I'd called him and Addy and asked them to come right over after I'd found it. Since my grandparents were out in the antique shop, we were talking in the front room. But I knew they could come in any minute, so we were whispering.

"I don't know," I told him. "I looked all around the porch, but I didn't see anybody."

"Did you show this to your grandparents?" Addy asked.

"No. They'd just get all worried," I told her and stuffed the note into my pocket. "They might even call my dad."

"So, what are you going to do about it?" she asked.

"Nothing, I guess, at least for now. Hey, my grandma told me all kinds of stuff about my grandpa, and the mine, and everything," I told them. "You won't believe some of what she said. But then she asked me not to ask any more questions around town or do anything that would be dangerous. That was the hard part."

Addy's eyes grew big. "You're not going to just give up, are you?"

"Of course not. It's just that I've always done what she's asked me to do – until now, I guess. Why don't we go upstairs to my room and talk?"

"Okay. You know, that was some creepy stuff Boone said yesterday, wasn't it?" David asked, raising his eyebrows. "I mean, talking about something keeping Ben alive? What did he mean by that?"

"It sounded mysterious to me," Addy said thoughtfully.

"Me, too," David said, puzzled. "I don't know if I believe what he said or not. I guess I don't really know what to think about it all."

"That's a first," Addy said with a grin. "Usually you try to pretend you know more about stuff than anyone else."

As we walked up the stairs, the strangest feelings swept over me. My hands and arms started tingling. The air suddenly felt colder, too. Something was happening.

My doorknob felt cold to the touch. Taking a deep breath, I turned it and opened the door. Then I just about stopped breathing.

"Oh... wow!" I heard David say behind me.

When my heart finally slowed down to nearly normal, I waved Addy and David into my room. "Come on in, you guys," I said.

My whole room was hazy; it almost looked like fog. Plus, it was really chilly. My regular old bedroom was transformed into some kind of different world!

The fog was so thick I could hardly see Addy or David, and they were standing right next to me. I couldn't make out anything else in the room.

Then, the fog lifted from the floor upwards. Amazingly, it revealed that Ben was standing there right in front of us. At first, he looked almost see-through, but he gradually got more solid and real. He had a dazed look on his face like he wasn't really sure where he was.

He was dressed like us, in a t-shirt, shorts, and shoes. Brown-eyed and brown-haired, he looked just like the picture we'd seen of him in the newspaper and like a younger version of his dad.

It felt like I was dreaming – where things could happen that couldn't usually happen in real life. I kept staring at him, taking in every detail, like seeing the thin strip of rawhide he wore around his neck. It held a dark arrowhead that had a hole pierced through the top. Or noticing the way he tied his shoes with double knots, just like I did.

It got so quiet in my room that the only sounds were that of my clock ticking and the four of us breathing.

Ben stared back at me. I could see fearfulness in his eyes as he looked at David and Addy and then around the room.

He stood up as if to run. "It's okay. These are my friends," I quickly told him. He nodded and sat back down.

I gazed over at David and Addy and saw that they looked as shocked and amazed as I felt right at that minute.

"I can't believe this is really happening," Addy suddenly said.

She walked over closer to Ben and finally reached out and touched his arm before quickly backing away again.

"It *is* pretty hard to believe," I said. Then, I took a deep breath. "We've got to promise not to tell anyone else. They'd never believe it, anyway. They'd just think we were crazy or something."

Both Addy and David nodded their heads solemnly. This would be our secret.

A few minutes passed with us staring at Ben and him staring at us.

Then David broke the silence, "Ben, now that you're here you can tell us what happened. We have lots of questions."

But Ben looked at him with a puzzled expression. "I don't remember much. It seems like I was just talking to my dad a few minutes ago."

That news hit me hard. I felt my arms start to shake.

"But that means...," Addy stopped in mid-sentence and looked over at me.

"It means he doesn't know what happened to him," I finished.

I sat down on the floor and leaned my back up against the wall. "Let's slow down. What's the last thing you remember, Ben?"

He got up and looked out the window. "I remember... that last day. My dad was having some problems with his boss, Mr. Roberts. He wouldn't tell me what it was, but I know he was worried about it."

"Was it something about the mine?" I asked, thinking back to what my grandparents had said about John Casey.

Ben turned back around. "I don't know. That afternoon my dad said we had to be prepared for anything. Then, later I heard a loud noise. That was the last day I remember being... well... alive."

He got a faraway look in his eyes. "It's all mixed up. Sometimes I feel like I just woke up from being asleep. I mean, it almost seems like it just happened. But, at other times it feels like it happened a long time ago."

"We'll try to help you," I said gently. "What do you want us to do?"

A flicker of sadness passed over his face. "I'd like to find my dad. I haven't seen him since that day."

He looked over at me. "Tyler, you have to help me," he begged. "You're my only hope. That's why I left that note for you."

I swallowed hard. The look of anguish on his face was painful to see. He looked totally lost and alone.

I turned to Addy and David and saw they were staring back at me with questioning looks. I had questions for them, too.

How in the world could I find Ben's dad?

CHAPTER EIGHT

We waited until after dinner when my grandparents drove away to visit some friends. That's when we took Ben to the quarry.

It was only a few minutes' walk from the back of the house, through a field of some sweet-smelling clover. I'd gone there many times over the years, but this was the first time I didn't plan to slide down to the bottom the second we got there. In fact, I didn't think I would do that ever again.

I kept looking around, afraid that someone we knew might spot us, and start asking questions about the brown-haired boy who was walking along with us.

"I hope no one sees us," I said. "How would we explain Ben?"

"The road is usually deserted by this time of day," Addy said. "I think we'll be okay."

"How does it work?" David asked, looking over at Ben. "You know. How do you appear or disappear?"

"You have a lot of questions," Ben said. He managed a

small grin. "But, I have more questions than you do. I don't even know why I'm still here."

I glanced over at him when he said that. For the first time, I saw a look of frustration cross his face. Right at that minute, I wished more than anything that I could somehow help him, although I had no idea how that would be possible. How could I reach back through time and find out what had happened to Ben and his dad?

As we walked, I heard animal noises all around us – dogs barking off in the distance, birds chirping, and frogs from the nearby pond croaking with their deep voices. While some creatures were quieting down for the day, others were waking up.

The daylight was fading as we got closer to where I'd found the skull and belt. I started to feel uneasy. The last time I was here, I'd found something that had turned my life upside down and kept me awake at night, wondering what to do about it.

I looked over at Ben, half-expecting him to look troubled or upset. But he didn't look bothered at all. He wore the same blank expression he had on his face most of the time, except when he talked. That's when he came to life.

This part of the quarry faced the ranch house. I remember never wanting to hang around here much because some beehives sat in the trees nearby. We could hear them buzzing and humming to our left.

"David, do you remember that time when you shot your slingshot at one of those beehives?" Addy asked.

"That was a long time ago. I wouldn't be fool enough to try that again," David fired back. "If we're telling tales on each other, I've got a few that Tyler might like to hear about you. What do you say to that?"

"Okay, okay, you guys," I told them. "Remember why

we're here."

"You're right. Sorry," Addy said.

"This place is huge," David said, walking closer to the edge and kicking a rock over the side with the toe of his shoe. "How could you find anyone buried here? You'd have to dig up the whole place."

Addy elbowed him in the ribs. "Real sensitive, aren't you?"

"What? It's true. Look around," David said, waving his hand out in front of him. "They've already dug all around the area where they found Ben. But his dad wasn't there."

As I looked out over the huge quarry, I saw that he was right. Where would you even start digging?

I looked at Ben. "I was hoping you'd feel something, if this was where... you know," I told him.

I didn't know how to finish the sentence. How do you talk to a ghost or spirit about where he died? I had no idea.

"It's okay," he said quietly. "You don't have to feel weird talking about it. I guess it happened a long time ago. The only thing I remember about the quarry is how much I used to play here with my friends."

Addy sighed and turned away. I knew exactly how she felt. It was hard not to like Ben and to feel sorry for what happened to him.

"Can we go over to my dad's workshop?" Ben suddenly asked, pointing to the antique shop.

"Sure, but it's changed now," I told him. "Grandpa said when he and Grandma moved into the ranch house, they found that someone had set fire to the shop."

"Who would do something like that?" Ben cried out. His eyes flashed with anger.

"He didn't know," I told him. "But at least the fire didn't completely destroy the place. Grandpa said it took months before the smell from the fire wasn't so awful anymore. Then, he built up the walls again and cleaned it all out."

When we were about twenty feet away from it, Ben started walking faster.

"What's up?" I asked, hurrying to catch up with him.

"I used to come here almost every day and watch my dad make things. He was a great carpenter," he said.

"He was a carpenter? I didn't know that," I told him.

I pulled open the door, which caused the bell overhead to ring. "It's all different now. My grandparents have changed it into an antique shop."

Ben entered right behind me while Addy and David trailed behind.

He walked around the room, looking at all the antiques hanging on the walls and lying on the shelves.

"It looks so different now. It used to smell like wood shavings. This was my dad's favorite place in the world," he said. "I used to help him make things sometimes. He could sand and stain two blocks of wood and when you put them next to each other you almost couldn't see there were two separate pieces. He could make hiding places, too."

"What kind of hiding places?" Addy asked, curious.

Ben grinned. "Well, he didn't like banks. So, he built a place inside a closet – I guess you'd call it a fake wall – where he kept his money and some other things."

Just then, the bell over the front door rang again. I looked up to see Jack and the guy we'd seen in his truck earlier.

I quickly turned around. Thankfully, Ben had already disappeared.

"Hey, guys. I promised your dad I'd come over and check on you, Tyler," Jack said. He nodded to his friend. "This is Sid. He and his family used to live in Dancing Creek, so I'm taking him around town, seeing how it's changed and all. He's visiting for a few days and working construction at the county fair."

After we said our hellos, Sid explored the crowded shop, looking at all the antiques.

Jack motioned to me that he wanted to talk, so we stepped back from the others.

"I've heard around town that you've been asking questions about the Casey's and Matthew Roberts," he said, giving me a hard look. "Your dad wouldn't want you doing that. What are you trying to do – solve a thirty-year-old case your grandpa couldn't solve?"

"Well... I was...," I started, but the look in his eyes stopped me from saying anything more.

"Just leave it be," he told me. With that, he turned and rejoined the others.

I stared after him, suddenly wondering if he was the one who had watched us with binoculars.

"You've got some great things here," Sid said. He stood in front of the ceiling-to-floor display case that was filled with all kinds of jewelry. "Some of these might be valuable."

"You think so?" David asked. He reached out his hand and inspected a few necklaces hanging from a stand on the counter. "It looks like a lot of junk to me."

"You would say that," Addy told him. "What do you know about jewelry?"

"Well, I guess you could say the same thing about me, too," Sid said with a laugh. "I really don't know anything about jewelry or antiques."

"My grandpa said a lot of it is costume jewelry. Those are things that are made up to look like real jewelry," I told him. "But there's also some things in there that my grandpa bought that are real."

After looking around the shop for a few minutes, Jack said, "We'd better get going. See you later."

Right after the door closed behind Jack and Sid, Ben reappeared.

"You got out of here just in time," David told him.

Ben nodded. "Yep. I get a feeling when someone is coming."

I stared out one of the windows, puzzled.

"What's the matter, Tyler?" Addy asked, walking over beside me.

"I'm sure now. I've seen Sid somewhere before," I told her.

But, it couldn't be, could it?

CHAPTER NINE

The next morning, Addy, David, and I rode our bikes into town to deliver some fair raffle tickets to my grandma's friend Cassie Winthrop. The county fair was this weekend, and my grandmother had asked Cassie to sell raffle tickets at the Dancing Creek Café. I figured it was the perfect chance to ask Cassie a few questions.

"Why do you have that look on your face?" Addy asked.

"Yeah. You look like a sick cow," David said with a grin.

"You should have seen my grandmother yesterday. She actually cried when she talked about when the Casey's disappeared and Grandpa couldn't solve the case. She's afraid I'll be in danger if I keep asking questions," I told them. "But, with Ben here now, I *have* to. I just feel bad about it. I've never lied to her before."

"Do you think she'll call your dad?" Addy asked, glancing sideways at me.

"Maybe. I sure hope not," I told her.

We biked along the beaten dirt path by the creek, shaded

by the leafy cypress trees that grew at the water's edge. The water was so clear here you could see the sandy bottom.

As we rode into town, I couldn't help thinking it still looked a lot like the frontier town it once was.

Two-block long Main Street was built extra wide for the cattle drives that were once driven straight through town. If I looked down the street and pretended the three cars weren't there, I could imagine cattle shoulder-to-shoulder, snorting and mooing, stirring up dust, and creating all kinds of noise and commotion.

The Dancing Creek Café stood halfway down Main Street, surrounded by saddle shops, western clothing stores, and a bank. Built out of weather-beaten wood, it had survived rain, sleet, snow, and wind for almost a hundred years. Grandpa called it an old-time relic – something from the past when cowboys hitched their horses out front and then stepped up to the wooden sidewalk in front of the café. Cassie Winthrop's grandparents had built the place. She'd worked there since she was a girl.

The smell of biscuits baking drifted up to us from the kitchen when I opened the door. Although it was still early yet, Alex, the cook, was probably hard at work in the kitchen.

Today, Cassie was sitting at her usual spot, next to the cash register up front. She'd told me once that she liked it there because she could watch the world go by outside and still keep an eye on her restaurant at the same time. She said that suited her just fine.

She looked the same as always, with her long hair piled high on her head, bright red lipstick on her lips, and wearing a white apron with "D.C. Café" stitched on it.

"Hi. How are you all doing?" she asked.

"Fine." I handed her the big roll of green fair raffle tickets. "My grandmother sent these. She said you were expecting them. Said she's already sold all of hers. I... guess you probably heard I found some things at the quarry."

Cassie nodded. "Sure did. Couldn't believe it when I first heard about it."

A worried look appeared on her face. "It's stirred up a lot of talk around here. Brings back some things that are hard to think about; ones I haven't thought about for years."

"You mean about John Casey and his son Ben?" Addy asked, leaning up against the front counter. "Did you know Ben at all?"

"Sure did. The town was really small back then, so we all knew each other. He was a good kid and was well-liked. I remember that he and his dad were always talking about fishing," she said with a smile. "And, when they weren't talking about fishing, they were *out* fishing."

Ben liked to fish? I loved to fish. That was another way we were alike.

Cassie settled back onto her stool. "That case was rough on your grandpa, Tyler. Plus, that mine owner, Matthew Roberts, gave your grandpa a hard time when he couldn't find the silver. He was a sly one, that man. There was something strange about him, but I could never put my finger on what exactly it was."

"We saw pictures of him in old newspapers at the library," I told her.

Cassie grinned. "He dressed like he was still in New York City, which was the only place he'd ever lived. He was sent out here because of some kind of family feud."

"Family feud?" I asked.

"That's right. He told me that himself," Cassie said. "He said he never got along with his family much, and he thought he was sent out here because of that. It was his father who actually owned the mine, and he asked John to run it."

"How did John Casey fit into that?" I asked.

"You mean with the mine? Well, he had mining experience. He'd worked at a mine out west before coming here," Cassie explained. "So, when the mine first opened, people around here were excited. But, after the robbery, everything changed."

"Hate to hear that whole mess being dug up again," one man said from a corner of the room.

"It's terrible, just terrible," another man added. "Why rake up all that stuff again?"

"I wouldn't worry too much about it. Nothing is going to come of it all. You'll see."

I turned around to see that it was Deputy Jack talking, as I'd thought. Great. Just great. Now Jack would probably call my dad, saying he'd heard I was asking questions about the case, after I'd been told not to.

Then, I had a worse thought. Dad had told me before he left to stay out of trouble, or we wouldn't go for our annual summer fishing trip out west.

Just then, the bell over the front door rang out, and a group of men walked in.

"That will be the start of my lunch crowd," Cassie said, getting up. "Be careful. Whoever did it could still be in town, and probably wouldn't want anyone looking into that business again."

Cassie headed toward the men with menus in her hand before I could ask her anything else.

When we got outside, David asked, "Wonder what happened to that silver? Maybe it's still hidden somewhere around here."

Addy rolled her eyes. "You're dreaming."

David glared back at her. "Well, it might be."

"Don't get any ideas," Addy told her brother. "If it was that easy to find, someone would have done it by now."

On the hot ride home, we took a break and walked close to the creek, under the shade of the cypress trees. Their roots looked like long toes, dangling over the bank into the water.

I tossed a stone into the water and watched it splash and then sink a short way to the bottom. "The creek is really low," I said.

David walked to the water's edge, dipped his hands in, and splashed his face. "Dad said that one year here it actually dried up."

Dried up. That's how I'd feel if my dad and I had to move, I thought.

But there was something else on my mind.

"I think Cassie wanted to say something else, until the other people started talking," I said.

"Well, she knew everyone involved in the case back then," Addy said. "Why? What are you thinking?"

I just shook my head. I wanted to wait until I found some proof about what I was thinking before I said anything.

CHAPTER TEN

I could tell right away that something was wrong when I opened the front door later that afternoon and saw the panicky look on Addy's face and realized that she was almost out of breath.

"I think David might be in trouble," she told me in a low voice, looking around to make sure we were alone. "We've got to do something."

We sat down on the front porch, where we often ended up when we didn't want to be overheard.

"What's he done this time?" I asked.

"I went into his room to see what he wanted to do this afternoon. He'd left me a note saying he was going to look for silver, out at the mine," she said, her eyes wide. "That's why I hurried over here."

"Slow down. Take a deep breath," I told her.

"I rode over here as fast as I could," she said, her eyes glistening with tears. She wiped some sweat from her forehead and then took a few deep breaths.

"Why does he think he might find silver there?" I asked her. "You mean the stolen silver shipment?"

"I don't know what he expects to find there. It's kind of my fault," she admitted. "Well, it *is* my fault. I teased him a bunch because he's always saying things that are crazy. Like when he said the silver might still be around here. Did he think he could find it, after people here had already searched everywhere for it? And, then it went on from there. You know how it is with us."

I sure did. Those two could argue about anything, and sometimes those arguments got hot.

"Okay. Let's fill up some canteens and I'll get my bike," I told her. "Hopefully, we can find him before he gets hurt or something."

I couldn't help thinking about the man who'd watched us by the creek or the threatening note I'd received. I wouldn't want to be all alone in an isolated spot right now. None of us were supposed to go way out somewhere alone, anyway. Trust David to do something that could get us all in trouble.

His parents would be sure to ask him why he went out there. I didn't think he'd tell them about Ben, but it could bring up questions I didn't want to answer.

"My uncle was talking to my mother on the phone this morning," Addy said after taking a drink of cool water from one of the canteens we were filling. "He told her this was the kind of weather that makes people do crazy things – because a big storm is headed our way."

I looked at her in surprise. "My grandma said something like that, too. It's like everything's changing outside and it makes the air funny. I guess it makes people act kind of crazy, too, although David's kind of like that anyway."

I glanced up at the sky. In just a few minutes, the weather had changed from sunny to being overcast. The clouds were moving fast and had blocked out the sun.

"The last big storm we got washed out the road by my house," Addy said.

"Flash floods are bad here," I told her. "They just get so big so fast that nothing much can stop them."

It didn't take us long to gather things up and head out. I had to pump the pedals of my bike hard to keep up with Addy, who was riding so fast her long hair flew out in back of her.

Addy and David were near impossible to figure out. They fought all the time, but when one of them needed the other, that person couldn't get there fast enough.

As we rode, I glanced from right to left. Tall weeds with small yellow flowers and prickly stickers lined the two-lane country road. Most of the trees had been cut down around here, leaving the bare ground to bake in the blazing sun.

When we rounded a final curve in the road, we saw a boarded-up opening at the bottom of the mountain ahead. It must have once been the mine entrance. I remembered seeing that picture of John Casey standing next to it.

"Hard to believe that silver came out of there," Addy said, looking around. "It's so ugly and... dead-looking."

That was it – the word I was looking for – dead.

We got off our bikes and walked toward the entrance, past a small wooden boxcar with only three wheels that tilted under the weight of rusty tools. Honeysuckle vines poked through a pile of broken boards, attracting buzzing bees with their sweet smell. Throughout the junk, fire ant mounds were scattered around. I knew if you stepped on a mound, dozens of ants would run out, ready to attack.

The entrance itself looked like a hole gouged out of the bottom of the mountain, covered with an iron gate. Behind the gate, a wooden door with the sign DANGER – DO NOT ENTER in faded red letters blocked our view.

"Look, there's David bike," Addy shouted. She pointed to the blue Schwinn that was leaning up against a part of an old fence post nearby.

I ran ahead and quickly spotted David. He was kneeling on the top of a hill to one side of the mine entrance. Even from where I was, I could see that his face was red, and sweat was pouring off it.

"What are you doing out here?" Addy shouted.

Surprised, David jumped up and stared at us in amazement. Then he shook his head, scampered down the hill, and walked over to where we stood.

"I was really mad, after you teased me. I rode out here because I knew you'd never been here. At least I could say I'd gone to the mine. But, once I got out here, it didn't seem like there was any easy way in," he admitted, looking down at the ground and not meeting his sister's eyes. "Guess I was kind of silly."

"Yeah – me, too," Addy said. She threw him a canteen.

David grabbed it from her and took a long gulp. Then he splashed some cool water over his face.

Suddenly Addy shivered. "Ever since we got here I've felt like someone was watching us."

David stood up. "I'll climb to the top of the hill. It's tall enough that I'll be able to see all around us."

"Just don't get hurt," Addy yelled.

We watched him scramble up the side of the hill. Every now and then, we could hear dirt crumbling away from the edge of where he was climbing.

Addy looked at David for a minute and then turned away. "I can't watch him anymore. Some day he's going to get hurt."

"Maybe you ought to come down," I shouted up to him. "You look like you're sliding around up there."

"Yeah - the dirt's all loose up here," David called from the hilltop. "Uh, the ground feels funny. It's kind of soft and…"

Suddenly David wobbled and fell to his knees. We heard a crumbling, rattling sound, and then he dropped down into the mine, completely out of sight.

CHAPTER ELEVEN

Addy and I raced up the hill. Halfway up, I stumbled and scraped my right knee on some rocks. The cut stung, but I got up and ran, trying to ignore the blood that was running down my leg. I'd deal with it later.

"Help!" David shouted from down inside the mine. "Get me out of here."

"David! Can you climb out?" Addy dropped to her hands and knees and crawled over to where her brother had disappeared. When she did, rocks and dirt crumbled down from the edge of the hole.

"Get back. It's not safe." I grabbed her arm and pulled her back. "It looks pretty deep down there, too."

"David, can you hear me? Are you okay?" Addy called, turning back to the hole.

"My right wrist hurts – a lot," he shouted. "I landed on it when I fell. It's dark and yucky in here. It's kind of wet, too."

I shivered even though the sun was hot on my back. There were probably snakes down there. This whole area was filled with rattlesnakes, and an old mine tunnel would probably make a good den. We had to hurry to get him out before one bit him. If that happened, he'd be in big trouble.

"How are we going to get him out of there?" Addy asked, with panic heavy in her voice. She turned around to face me. "He's down there too deep to climb out."

"I-I can't breathe," David cried out. "Help!"

"We're going to get you out to fresh air as fast as we can. Calm down. Take slow, deep breaths," I told him.

"I've got an idea." Addy jumped up and ran down the hillside, her shoes pounding the ground so hard the sounds echoed up the hill.

"Okay, I'm better," David yelled. "It's just that I can hear noises in here. It sounds like something is crawling around."

I groaned, imagining a rattlesnake sliding towards David. I didn't know much about snakes, but I had a pretty good idea that one would defend its den. I didn't want to start talking about snakes being down there, though. That would just make him more scared than he already was.

Addy ran back, holding her bike light in one hand. "We can use this for a flashlight. I took it off my bike."

I grinned at her. "Smart. Now, shine it down on David."

We crawled as close to the hole as we dared, stopping when dirt and dust again started crumbling down. Then, Addy focused the light on her brother.

I saw David sitting on the floor of the tunnel, looking up at us. He held his right wrist in his left hand.

"Can you stand up?" I asked.

"I think so." He slowly stood up and looked around him. "Get me out of here, okay?"

"Let's go back down to the mining stuff," Addy suggested. "Maybe we can find something to help get him out."

She ran ahead of me downhill, and I followed as fast as I

could, trying not to think how scary it would be down there alone at the bottom of the mine in the darkness.

We ran over to where the old mining equipment tools sat in the overgrown grass and weeds. The sweet smell of the honeysuckle and the buzzing of the bees almost overwhelmed me as I walked right into the middle of them.

"We've got to be careful," I told Addy. "Besides the bees and the fire ants, anything could be underneath or inside some of this old stuff."

"You mean like snakes?" she asked, looking around. "Small snakes are okay, but I don't like big ones."

"Me neither." There was a big difference between looking at a rattlesnake in a cage or behind some glass and having one rattle his tail at you from a foot away when you poked through the weeds.

Addy went one way, and I went the other. Could we find something we could use to help get David out of the mine in all of this junk?

I tested the ground with the toe of my shoe before I stepped down anywhere. Some of the higher weeds reached over my knees. A few reached up to my shoulders. Those were the worst. I felt like I was walking through a minefield.

Just then, I remembered my grandma's words about not doing anything dangerous. I hoped she'd never find out about this. If we all got out of this as I hoped, she never would.

I got a big stick and poked around, careful to stay away from the huge fire ant mounds. I saw something coiled up underneath the wagon. I walked toward it slowly, and then I got down on my knees and poked it with the stick. Nothing. I stuck my head under the wagon and took a good look. It wasn't a snake at all. It was a length of rope.

I pulled it out. It was old and ratty looking, but it was still in one piece.

Addy made a face. "Yuck! It stinks and it's got all kinds of bugs and spider webs and stuff on it."

"Come on!" I grabbed the coil of rope and ran. I knew that every second David was down in the mine tunnel, something could be crawling toward him in the darkness.

Back at the top of the hill, Addy and I tied knots in the rope every few feet. It was lucky it was David down there. Out of all of us, he had the best chance of getting out. He was the lightest, and he loved to climb.

Finally, I got up and went back over to the hole. "Get back, David. We're going to try to widen the hole a little. Then, we're going to drop a rope down and see if you can climb up on it."

"Okay," David answered. "Just hurry up, okay?"

Addy and I got some big sticks and pushed around the sides of the hole. Some spots gave way easily, while others wouldn't budge. We had to be careful because we didn't know if the ground we were standing on would collapse at any minute.

"I sure hope this works," Addy said. "If it doesn't, I'm going for help."

Together we pulled the rope over to the hole and dropped one end of it down.

"Grab hold of the rope," I shouted down to David. "Hold on as tight as you can. We're going to try to pull you up, but we need you to try to help us, too."

I braced myself as best as I could. "Okay, David."

Seconds later, I felt a tug on the other end and knew David had grabbed onto it. Slowly I pulled the rope up, just a little. My arms ached with the strain. I pulled some more.

As I did, I heard scraping noises from down below. That was encouraging.

"Let me help." Addy grabbed the rope behind me and pulled, too.

We worked together without a word. Every now and then, one of us would groan with the effort. We could only pull a little at a time.

It seemed to take forever until we first saw David, holding tight to the rope, stick his head out of the hole. If I hadn't been so tired, I would have yelled out loud; I was so glad to see him.

A few strong tugs later, Addy and I pulled him up and over the edge of the hole. We all ended up in a tangled heap.

David sat up and dusted some of the dirt and rocks off himself with his left hand. He held his right arm still.

"How's your wrist?" I asked.

"It hurts, but it'll be okay. It has to be."

"What do you mean by that?" Addy asked while trying to pull some sticker weeds off her socks.

He looked at us about as seriously as I'd ever seen him. Then he said, "You both have to promise me you won't tell anyone we were ever here."

CHAPTER TWELVE

"Dad said he'd ground me the next time I got into trouble," David said. "If he does, I'll miss the slingshot contest this weekend." He kicked a rock and sent it flying down the hillside, along with a shower of dust, until it hit the bottom with a thud. "That would mean I'd practiced a whole year for nothing. A whole year!"

Addy stared at him in disbelief. "You need a doctor to look at your wrist. Besides, Dad will find out anyway."

"He won't find out if you guys don't tell him," David said. He looked down at his right hand. "My wrist hardly hurts anymore."

"It would be silly to try and keep it a secret, if your wrist is really hurt," I told him. "You have to do something about it."

"Well, I guess I'm silly, then," David said, his voice rising. A stubborn look settled on his face. "Anyway, it's my wrist, so it should be my choice."

"Go ahead and do whatever you want. That's what you usually do, anyway," Addy said, glaring at her brother.

"It's not right to ask us to lie for you," I told him, my voice rising too, although I was trying to stay calm.

"I thought you were my friend," David shouted. "I guess I was wrong."

He pushed past us and ran down the hill, brushing up against bushes and kicking up dust along the way. He held his head high and didn't look back.

Addy wiped some sweat from her forehead with the back of one hand. "Dad expects me to watch out for him and keep him out of trouble. But, if I try to tell David anything he yells at me. Then, he goes off and does something stupid."

I nodded in sympathy. "That's not fair. You ought to talk to your parents and tell them that."

"I've told them that before, but they never listen. They say I'm the oldest, so I should watch out for him." She tried to smile, but it came out sad-looking. With a shrug, she started walking down the hill.

I hurried downhill and caught up with them by the bees buzzing around the honeysuckle. David looked so mad I was afraid for the bees. Addy's red face and pinched look told me to forget what I'd planned to say to try to make her feel better. It would take more than that.

Before we took off on our bikes, we grabbed our canteens and took long, cool drinks. Then I poured water onto my cut knee and tried to wipe some of the blood and dirt off.

We pedaled back single file, with David in the lead and me bringing up the rear. My knee hurt every time I bent it, so I rested that foot on the middle of the bike frame and let my other foot push the bike pedal up and down.

When we got to the turn in the road where we went separate ways, I'd already made up my mind about what I'd say. "I'm not going to tell my grandparents we went to the mine. I'll see you guys later."

When I got home, I went to the barn and got out the first aid kit my grandparents kept there in one of the cabinets. Just as I opened it, I heard a creaking noise somewhere behind me, I whirled around, but there was nothing there. Guess I was just jumpy.

Turning back around, I gritted my teeth for what I knew would hurt. I dropped some stinky antiseptic onto my cut knee. It stung and stung some more, just like I knew it would. Then, I stuck a bandage on it and hoped no one would notice.

I ran up the stairs to my room and changed clothes. Later, when I walked into the kitchen and my grandparents looked up at me, I tried to act like nothing had happened. Keeping the secret about going to the mine and David getting hurt was hard. But I didn't want to get David into any trouble.

"Everything okay, Tyler?" my grandmother asked. She was shelling peas, and every time she snapped a pod open, the peas tumbled out into her bowl. She bent forward, looking concerned. "How'd you hurt your knee?"

"Oh, I tripped and scraped it," I said, turning away from her to smell some flowers that sat in a vase on the table. I was careful not to look into her eyes. If I did, she could probably tell right off that I wasn't telling the truth – the whole truth, that was.

"Your dad called," Grandpa announced.

"What did he say?" I asked nervously, half-holding my breath.

He paused a minute to draw out the suspense. Then, he smiled widely. "The District Chief said he thought he was needed here. You two won't have to move. They're going to keep him up there a few more days. Then, he's coming home."

"That's great," I told him, with a big smile of my own and a ton of relief flooding through me.

"Why don't we celebrate by eating dinner tonight at the

Café?" Grandpa suggested. "I feel like having some spicy enchiladas."

"Sounds good," I told him.

Later, on the ride there, I thought again about David yelling at Addy and me. I hoped we could still be friends. But you never knew with David. Sometimes he could be a crusty crab.

The café was packed for dinner. My grandparents waved to friends as Cassie took us to our favorite table, next to a back wall under a collection of old cowboy boot spurs. It was quieter there, and you could talk without having to shout over the sound of the laughter and talk around you.

Grandpa and I ordered enchiladas with peach cobbler for dessert. My grandmother chose the chicken potpie with the flaky crust, along with homemade vanilla ice cream.

Cassie took our orders and gave them to Alex, the cook. Afterward, she sat down to visit with us.

"We're going to get that weather soon," Grandpa predicted. "This might be a big one, too, from what I've heard. Keep an eye on the sky when you're out, Tyler."

Around here, when someone said you were going to *get weather,* you could bet it wasn't going to be the good kind. Tonight Grandpa would probably go all around the house and the antique shop, shutting things up and moving outside things into the barn so they wouldn't get blown away.

"So, how'd you meet John Casey, anyway?" I asked Grandpa while we were waiting for our food.

He took a long drink of his iced tea before answering. "I met him because your grandmother worked with his wife, Emily, for a year before Emily died. After that, he just seemed to want to get away from here as fast as he could. We made an offer to buy the ranch and Casey accepted it. Not long afterwards, he and Ben disappeared."

"Emily Casey was a teacher," my grandmother added, pouring some cream into her coffee. "We taught at the same school. She was a wonderful person. Emily was just starting out teaching and wanted to do everything right. I tried to help her. Then, she got sick suddenly, and her cancer finally killed her."

"When did she die?" I asked.

"Right around the time the silver was stolen," Cassie answered. She shook her head. "She'd had a hard life, with those crazy outlaw brothers and all."

"Outlaw brothers?" I asked, thinking I hadn't heard her right.

Cassie nodded. "Her father built your grandparents' ranch, Tyler. Emily and her brothers Nathan and Thomas grew up there. Those two were always getting into trouble of some sort, and finally ended up in prison after robbing some banks."

She stopped for a minute when a waitress came to their table loaded down with big platters of great-smelling food, which she passed out to us.

Then, Cassie continued. "After her parents died, Emily and John moved into the ranch house. Things looked like they were finally going to ease up for her. But, then she got sick. Her brothers broke out of prison shortly after she died."

I looked at my grandparents in astonishment.

"You never told me they actually lived in the ranch house – the brothers I mean. I read about them at the library," I told them.

"That's not something we liked to talk about," Grandma admitted

"They were killed in a shootout down south a few weeks after they escaped," Grandpa added, as he dropped a spoonful of sugar into his tea and stirred it in, clicking the spoon against the side of the glass. "Over the years since then, we've tried to put it behind us. Believe me, it was awful around here at the time."

"What was Matthew Roberts like?" I asked Cassie. "Did you talk to him much?"

"Sure. About a year after he came to town his wife got tired of living here and took their kids and went back to New York," Cassie said. "I can't say I liked the man, but I couldn't help feeling sorry for him."

"Why?" I asked, taking another crunchy taco chip from the straw basket on the table.

"He didn't belong here. He never fit in, and there were also all kinds of rumors about him. Some claimed his family sent him out here just to get rid of him. Those kinds of things wear a person down."

I'd thought Matthew Roberts would be happy because he owned a silver mine. Guess that hadn't helped him much.

"The only thing he liked was collecting diamonds and antiques. Plus, can you imagine being used to living in New York City, and then coming to hole-in-the-wall Dancing Creek?" Cassie asked. "He was lost here."

I'd never been to New York, but I'd seen enough pictures to know there was a world of difference between here and there.

Thinking all this over, I spooned some of the orangery-red enchilada sauce from my plate over an enchilada. Then, I added two small jalapeño slices on top. Perfect. One mouthful combined the sensation of a creamy, cheesy sauce, soft corn tortilla, and a mild jolt of warmth that spread to my nose and throat.

We left the café and went home soon afterward. But I couldn't get Cassie's words out of my head.

When I closed my eyes to go to sleep that night, her words about Matthew Roberts echoed in my head. *Lost. Lost. Lost.*

CHAPTER THIRTEEN

I woke up early the next morning with one thought. Today I would look for proof of my suspicions. There was only one place where I thought I might find it.

After eating breakfast, I ran out the front door, eager to get started. But, once again, I saw a note, sitting on the front porch, held down by a rock.

I stopped at once. Whoever was doing this was getting bolder. This note was right next to the door, close to a big window.

"This is your last warning" was written in big, bold letters.

I looked all around, but I didn't see anyone. So, I turned back and read the note again. Like it or not, I knew I should probably tell my grandparents and Deputy Jack about it. But I'd put it off as long as I could.

I stuffed the note into my pocket for now. I hoped I wasn't making a mistake by not telling anyone about it.

Then, I took a deep breath, got on my bike, and headed into town to the museum. I knew it kept old papers and pictures. On the way, I thought about all I'd learned in the past few days about the Casey's, Matthew Roberts, and the events of the past, trying to put it all together.

The museum looked the same as always – a long, one-story building built out of limestone blocks. In the yard stood a huge old pecan tree whose branches were covered with lime green leaves that fanned up and down in the breeze. I bet its pecans would make a great pie.

My first stop inside was always the stuffed two-headed baby goat because it was so creepy looking. No matter which direction you walked, one of its four brown eyes would stare at you like it was still alive.

The town museum was filled with farm tools, long guns, and sharp knives with carved handles that pioneers used to settle Dancing Creek. Whenever I looked at them, I wondered what kind of pioneer I would have made. I knew you had to be strong and tough to last very long out here.

I found Mrs. Jennings, the lady who ran the museum, dusting the top of an exhibit case. She liked to say that she was so wrinkled she could be one of the exhibits herself. That always made me laugh.

"Hello, Tyler." She smiled and set down her dusting cloth and can of lemony-smelling wax. "Everyone in town is talking about what you found. I have to say that was pretty amazing, finding those things after all this time. You must have sharp eyes."

"That's what people tell me," I said. "I guess I'm just always looking around. I'm here because I wanted to find out more about Ben."

"I don't know if I have any information about him, but if we do it will be in the file about the silver mine. Follow me."

I followed her and her sharp clicking steps until she stopped before an old silvery gray filing cabinet. "Anything we have on the mine would be in the first drawer."

I pulled open the top drawer of the cabinet and looked inside. There was a large stack of old newspapers there. Everything had a musty been-there-forever kind of smell that tickled my nose. I bet no one had taken them out and looked at them in a long time, just like the papers in the library.

It didn't take me long to find some articles about the mine opening in Dancing Creek. It was big news for a small town. I unfolded one yellowed paper, smoothed it out with my hand, and looked at a picture of the wealthy Roberts family from back East, the paper said. The men wore suits and ties. The women wore long fancy dresses and pearl necklaces.

Then, I suddenly got what Grandpa would have called a *brainstorm*. Well, it was either a brainstorm or the craziest idea in the world. But the longer I thought about it, the more it actually made a lot of sense.

What if Cassie was right, and Matthew Roberts' family *had* sent him here to this dusty Texas town to get rid of him? He probably would have been mad. Maybe he'd even been mad enough to do things that would eventually shut down the mine. Then, he could go back to New York, to his wife and children. Plus, he could take the antiques and diamonds he had collected with him.

Suddenly I heard footsteps coming my way. They didn't sound like Mrs. Jennings' sharp clicking ones.

Addy stepped around a display case. "Hi, Tyler. Your grandmother said you were here."

She looked at the papers piled on the top of the file cabinet. "Have you found anything there?"

"I was looking at this picture of Matthew Roberts' family." I held the newspaper up for her to see.

"The people don't look real friendly, do they?" she observed. "They don't even look as if they like each other."

I'd noticed that, too. In most family pictures I'd seen, the people were smiling and maybe had their arms around each other. Not in this picture.

There was also a box at the bottom of the drawer. We lifted it down to the floor. Inside I found a few pictures of the mine, and also some pictures of Matthew Roberts' house here and its furnishings. Even though he'd moved to a tiny town, he'd furnished it like an elegant house in New York.

Addy pointed to a picture of the Roberts' dining room, which had a crystal chandelier hanging down from the ceiling. "That's pretty fancy for Dancing Creek. It's hard to imagine anyone having that here."

That was true. But the longer I looked at it, the more I was sure that I'd seen it before. But where? Then I remembered Grandpa saying he'd bought some things from Matthew Roberts' estate sale. I'd have to ask him about it.

As we were about to put everything back in the box, I saw one more paper at the bottom. With a hopeful feeling, I pulled it out and opened it. I couldn't believe my eyes when I saw what I'd come here to find – pictures of the outlaw brothers.

I looked closer. "Hey, Addy," I called out, pointing to the picture. "Look at this guy on the right. Does he remind you of anyone?"

Addy studied the picture and then drew back with a surprised look on her face. "Tyler, he looks just like Sid, that guy who came to your grandparents' shop with Jack."

I stared at the picture once again. The eyes were the same in both men. Plus, they both had the same blond hair, parted to one side.

Could they be father and son? Did Sid come back to Dancing Creek to get the money his dad and uncle had stolen from banks, and which lawmen never found?

CHAPTER FOURTEEN

After Addy and I biked back to the ranch, we went into the kitchen, drank some cold lemonade, and planned what to do next. My grandparents were out at the fairgrounds, along with Addy and David's parents, working on last-minute details, so we were alone.

"I found this on the porch this morning," I told her and showed her the note.

"Who could be doing this?" she asked. She looked up at me with fear in her eyes. "Maybe you should have told your grandparents about it."

"If I had, they'd never have let me go to the museum and we wouldn't have seen that picture. I'll tell them as soon as I can," I told her and took the note back.

"Your grandmother made everything in there, didn't she?" Addy asked, nodding toward a box sitting on the kitchen table.

Inside were rows of shiny glass canning jars filled with corn, green beans, tomatoes, and peas. There was also a huge jar of her all-you-can-eat pickles, sitting by itself on the counter. We called them that because one pickle was so long and round that it filled you up. I'd never heard anyone ask for a second one.

"Yep. They're for the canning contest at the fair," I told her, staring out the window at the sky, which was growing darker.

"The wind's picking up pretty fast. You can already hear it blowing," Addy said.

"Alanna," I called, suddenly realizing that she hadn't come rushing up to me the minute I got home. Where was she?

I went out and opened the back door and whistled for her. But there was no answer. I finally shut the door and walked back into the kitchen. Something was wrong. I knew it.

Just then, Ben appeared in front of us, once again appearing first as a faint outline and then becoming more solid. I'd wondered when he was going to show up. It seemed that Boone was right. Ben couldn't leave the property here.

I told him about the picture we'd seen at the museum. "The two brothers were your uncles – Nathan and Thomas. Do you remember hearing their names?"

Ben's eyes narrowed as he thought about it. "I think so. I heard my parents talking one day, saying the two were away somewhere."

"They were sent to prison," Addy told him.

Ben nodded. "That's right. I remember now. I think my mother was afraid of them, especially Nathan. He could be real mean. That bothered my dad a lot."

"What did he think would happen?" Addy asked.

"Nothing good," Ben assured us. "I'm remembering more things now. Dad started a journal. He said if anything happened to him, people could read it and the record would be set straight. But I don't know where he kept it."

"Sounds like there could be important information in it," I

said.

"Do you think it could still be here after all this time?" Addy asked.

"Who knows, but it's worth looking for it," I said. "I've got an idea. Let me show you something."

I went over to a cupboard and looked through some papers. Then, I took one out and returned to the table.

"These are the building plans for this house," I told her, spreading the paper out flat with my hands. "Grandpa showed it to me once. It shows the layout of all the rooms."

I pointed to one place on the drawing. "This is the front room. For some reason, there's an X marked on it. There's also an X marked on Grandpa's study. Grandpa said he didn't put the X's there."

I looked up at her. "I think we should search both of those places. Ben said his dad made hiding places."

"Sure. Let's do it," Addy said, looking hopeful.

"The X's are in the corners of the room, where people wouldn't go too often," I told her.

Addy nodded. "They would probably make good places to hide things."

I led her into the front room, which we never used much. Then, I went to the front left corner. "You lift the other side of this rug, okay?"

My heart was beating fast as I moved a small brown table out of the area we were going to search. Then, I pulled back the edge of the woolen rug that covered the floor.

At the same time, Addy pulled the rug back from her corner of the room.

"Listen," she suddenly said. "It's starting to rain."

"It's the start of that big storm," I said, hearing the drops splatter against the house. "I bet my grandparents will be stuck out at the fairgrounds for a while. Okay. Now, shine your flashlight on the floor. See if there's anything there, like a trap door, or something you can pull open, some kind of hiding place."

Addy shot me a questioning look, but she did what I asked.

I did the same thing where I was, lowering my head down until it was just a few inches from the floor. To my amazement, I saw lines there. Maybe there was something underneath them.

"Addy, come look at this," I said.

"What do you think it is?" she asked, looking over my shoulder.

"Well, it's not very big – barely two feet wide. I'll get some tools and see if we can pry this wood up."

It didn't take me long to find some chisels and race back there. After about fifteen minutes, we managed to pry the wooden top off.

"It's empty," Addy announced.

"Okay," I told her with a sigh. "Let's put everything back and try my grandpa's study next."

A few minutes later, we went to his study and tried again, moving small tables and even Grandpa's big vanilla-smelling candle from his desk. Then we pulled back the rug at the corners of the room. As we worked, we could hear the rain sprinkling steadily outside.

We saw the exact same thing when we looked under the rug in the study. There were lines in the floor again. So, we pried the wood up. But, once again, we stared down into an empty space.

"You know," I told her. "Maybe these are hiding places the brothers used to hide the things they stole. Let's put everything back."

We silently moved everything back into place and then went back to sit at the dining room table again. I felt disappointed that we hadn't found anything, but I wasn't going to give up. Not now.

I thought for a while and then asked, "What do we know about Ben's dad?"

"He knew all about carpentry – woodworking," Addy said. "If his wife hadn't died, they probably would have had more kids."

"Those kids might even have kids of their own by now, running around the house or asleep in the nursery," I told her.

"What nursery?" Addy asked.

"It's that small room upstairs, across from my room," I explained. "My grandparents use it mostly to store things. But they still call it the nursery. Come on. I'll show you. I haven't gone in there in a long time."

We all got up and walked upstairs. I felt incredibly nervous for some reason. Maybe it was because I could hear the storm building up outside and knew it would only get louder. Maybe it was because my head was bursting with all the information we'd found out, and I was trying to make sense of it all.

The nursery was the last room at the end of the long hallway upstairs. When I opened the door, there was the same kind of smell as the file cabinet drawer in the museum. The curtains were shut tight to keep out the summer heat. I flicked the light on.

"Look, Tyler!" Addy cried out. "Is that the chandelier we saw in the picture at the museum – the one that used to belong to Matthew Roberts?"

Staring up at the shimmering crystal object hanging from the ceiling, I felt a tingling feeling run down my back. Yes – it looked like the one I'd seen before, long ago.

"This must be one of the things Grandpa bought from Matthew Robert's estate sale," I told her. "Let's get it down."

I stood on a chair and unhooked it from where it hung.

With Addy's help, I lowered it to the floor. Then, I examined it all around.

"What are you doing?" Addy asked. "Can I help?"

I grinned at her. "Well, I could be all wrong, but I think Matthew Roberts might have stashed some diamonds in here."

"Diamonds?" Addy asked doubtfully.

"Cassie said he collected diamonds and antiques. He may have been stealing money from the mine to buy them. See, I think he was trying to build up the idea that the mine wasn't making enough money to stay open. He wanted to shut it down," I told her.

By that time, Addy was running her hands over the top of the chandelier like I was. There were some metal openings there that weren't shut all the way, like the others.

I went and got a screwdriver and pried one of them open. Something lay cradled inside.

"Looks like a diamond," I said, pulling it out. "I don't know for sure if it's real or not."

Addy held it up to the light and turned it this way and that.

"Look how it sparkles and shines," she said. "I bet it's a real diamond alright. I don't think a fake one would do that."

"Let's leave it here until Grandpa comes back. He's going to be amazed," I told her.

Ben looked around. "I remember this room. My dad built the bed, and the table and chairs, too."

As soon as he said that, I got an idea. I turned and looked around the room for any type of wood with a pattern in it, where you could slide one piece of wood over another. The only wood I could find like that was the wooden bed frame right behind my head. I ran my hand slowly over the side.

I pushed one wooden section up and then down. Nothing happened. I looked closer at the wood. Then, I pressed my whole hand against the wood and pushed hard. Finally, I heard a click and felt a panel of the wood move.

The secret compartment was less than a foot long. It seemed simple when it was open, but I bet that it was harder to make than it looked. The sliding part had to slide in and out perfectly and fit into the pattern on the bed frame.

Tucked inside was a small brown leather notebook.

CHAPTER FIFTEEN

We got plenty of thunderstorms here, so we were used to their loud booms and shakes. But this didn't sound anything like a normal storm. The crashing and groaning felt like it was right in the house with us.

"The wind must be terrible outside," Addy said, raising her voice so she could be heard over the storm. "It's shaking the whole house."

I nodded. "I've never heard the windows rattle like this before. Hope one doesn't blow out."

"I can't ever remember a storm this bad," Addy said.

"Me either," I told her. "You won't be able to leave for a while until it lets up."

Seconds later, the rain built up to a roar and pounded the roof and sides of the house with a new fury. I crawled to the window and parted the curtains. The wind was ripping branches from the trees and smashing them against the house. Then I heard a sound like a lion's muffled roar. It quickly grew louder as if coming closer.

Addy and I looked at each other questioningly. Was this a tornado? Grandpa had talked about one day building a storm shelter. I'd have to remind him about that.

It sounded like something alive was out there, trying to get in. Addy finally put her head down and shoved her hands over her ears.

Ben alone looked untouched. I guessed he was beyond the reach of something as alive as this storm.

The worst storms here lasted about an hour. But, that time had come and gone. Right now, the waves of wind and rain hitting us were getting stronger instead of letting up.

Suddenly, all the lights blinked and then went out. That left us in darkness, waiting for whatever was going to come next. A tremendous flash of lightning lit up the sky. Seconds later, rumbling thunder shook the house under us and rattled everything in the room. The storm was throwing everything it had at us.

Finally, I said, "We don't have any flashlights up here. Let's go downstairs. At least we'll have some light then."

Addy stood up, and we slowly made our way downstairs, holding onto the stair railing all the way. Ben trailed behind us silently.

We found the flashlights and went into the kitchen. There we sat, with our flashlights sitting on the table, focused on us. It was eerie looking, with our faces barely lit up, in an otherwise dark room.

"I forgot to tell you," Addy suddenly said. "David ended up having to go to the doctor after all. Mom spotted the problem he was having with his wrist right away."

I shook my head. "I knew he wouldn't be able to keep it a secret. Did he get into trouble?"

"Not really. Dad said he'd been punished enough, because he had to get it all wrapped up, and can't enter the contest now."

"That's too bad," I told her. "He probably would have won."

"Do you think David will ever get better?" Addy asked in a low voice. "You know what I mean."

"Yeah. He can't get any worse," I said with a grin.

She laughed at that, and I joined in with her.

It felt good to lighten things up. For the last few hours, I'd fought against an overwhelming feeling that something bad was going to happen. I'd never felt this way before, so it was bewildering. My insides felt like the weather outside.

I could hear the rain still beating against the house while the wind kept up its howling. If I could find something to do, then maybe I wouldn't feel so jittery.

I held the worn leather journal out to Ben. "Do you want to read it out loud? After all, it's your dad's book."

He shook his head. "I'll just listen."

"Here, I'll read it," Addy said. She took the book and aimed her flashlight over it. "Look how small the writing is."

The small letters in black ink stood out boldly against the background of the white-lined pages.

"I'm going to start toward the end," she told us, paging through the small book. "That's probably what we're most interested in."

After scanning a few pages, she started reading.

"I've been keeping an eye on Mr. Roberts for a while now and know that something's not right. I finally told him today I thought he was stealing money from the mine, and that I planned to tell the sheriff," she read. "I'm not sure if there was ever any stolen silver shipment at all."

"That's what I was thinking," I burst in. "Roberts needed some kind of way to explain the money that was missing from the mine, because he'd stolen it to buy antiques and diamonds."

"I wonder if anyone thought of that at the time," Addy said, looking over at me, clutching the journal in her hands.

I shrugged. "I don't know. Maybe people didn't think the owner of a business would do something like that. Mr. Casey was probably the only one close enough to Mr. Roberts to realize what he was doing. So, he'd be the perfect person for Mr. Roberts to blame."

Just then, a deep boom of thunder exploded like a cannon. It brought us out of our thoughts and back to wanting to know what was in the journal.

"Keep reading," I said. "Don't stop now."

"The next entry is dated a few days later," she said. "Roberts has threatened me, saying he'll kill Ben if I tell the sheriff what I know. What kind of a monster would kill a boy?"

Upon hearing that, I glanced over at Ben. He'd grabbed onto the edge of the table with both hands as if to steady himself. More than anything else, he looked astonished.

Addy pushed the diary across the table. "Here, Tyler. You read it. It's creepy reading someone else's diary. It's sad, too."

I picked up the diary and found the next entry. "My beloved wife has been dead a month now. I don't want to stay in Dancing Creek anymore. It would be better to start my life over far away."

Then, I skipped down to the last entry. "I've just heard that Emily's brothers have broken out of prison. They've always hated me – saying I'd turned her against them. Hopefully, Ben and I will be gone from here in a few days. That way, we'll stay safe from them. But they're evil – and I fear if they get the chance they will take revenge on Ben and me because of Emily's death."

I stared down at the last line for quite a while. I could easily picture John Casey sitting alone and writing that while desperately trying to figure out a way to keep himself and Ben alive. The worry and strain must have been overwhelming.

When I finally looked up, Ben had disappeared.

"So, what do you think happened? Who shot Ben?" Addy asked in a low voice.

A whirlwind of thoughts and images flashed through my head. I saw Matthew Roberts in his fancy clothes, holding a gun in one hand. Then, I pictured Nathan and Thomas, the outlaw brothers, racing toward Dancing Creek on fast horses.

Who got there first?

CHAPTER SIXTEEN

During one of the brief periods of calm in between onslaughts from the storm, I heard a noise by the front door. I motioned to Addy to stay quiet while I peeked around the corner into the entryway.

I saw Jack's friend Sid fighting the wind and blowing rain and finally managing to close the door behind himself. His clothes were dripping wet, and his hair was plastered down on his head. Just like us, he held a flashlight to light his way.

Once inside, he tore off his wet jacket and threw it on the ground. Then, he shook his head back and forth, flinging water this way and that.

He wasn't smiling anymore. The friendly look was gone, too. His eyes were cold, like those of a wolf. I guessed that this was the *real* Sid but that he could change like a chameleon as quickly as a snap of the fingers.

He headed down the hallway. I took my shoes off and got ready to follow him, with Addy right behind me. We had to wait until he walked into Grandpa's study because there was nowhere to hide in the narrow hall. Then we tiptoed to just outside the door, where we could watch him.

He aimed the beam of his flashlight from left to right over the top of my grandpa's desk while looking at the papers there.

"What's he doing?" Addy whispered.

"I don't know."

Sid must have heard us because he suddenly jerked around and aimed his flashlight at us. Then, he pulled a black gun from his pocket. "Come over here, you two!"

Behind me, I heard Addy gasp. I swallowed hard and stood up.

"What's going on?" I asked. "What are you doing here?"

Rain dripped down Sid's forehead. He wiped it away impatiently with the back of one hand.

"Think I'm doing this because I want to? I need to pay back some money I owe for gambling, real bad, to people who get angry when they don't get their money on time," he told me.

"So – are you looking for the money your dad stole years ago?" I asked, watching to see his response.

Sid's eyes narrowed as he scowled. "So, you know about that, do you? No – I don't know what happened to it. My guess is that someone found it a long time ago and has kept quiet about it for all these years. That's not why I'm here."

At that, Addy walked over and stood at my side. She threw a quick, nervous glance over at me before concentrating her attention on Sid.

Once again, he wiped away some water dripping down his forehead with his hand.

"Where's your grandpa's antique book? The one where he keeps all his records?" he demanded.

"Why do you want that?" I asked, staring at the gun.

"Just get me the book!" Sid shouted, waving the gun at me. "I don't have time for chit chat."

Feeling that I had no other choice, I walked over to the bookcase and pulled out the heavy binder. I struggled to rope in my senses, which were reeling.

Sid snatched it from my hands. He lugged it back to the desk and opened it.

"You said you didn't know anything about antiques," I said, watching him page through the book, where Grandpa had kept careful records. Each page contained a description, told where he'd gotten the antique and how much he'd paid for it.

"I lied. I know that your grandpa has some valuable antiques that once belonged to Matthew Roberts. There was even a rumor that he'd hidden diamonds in some of the pieces. I have someone all lined up who will buy them, no questions asked. After I sell them, I'll have enough money to pay off my debts and leave this town forever," he said, emphasizing the last part of the sentence.

"Isn't there anyone you could ask for a loan, so you don't have to do this?" I asked.

Sid laughed in my face. "No, kid. It's too late for that."

"What about Jack? Does he know who you really are, or why you're doing this?" Addy asked him.

"Nah. I just met him a few weeks ago, and pumped him for information," Sid said, not even bothering to look up from the book. "My cousin already had told me about the antiques, especially the ones from Matthew Roberts. Those are the ones I want."

I brushed Addy's hand with my fingers to get her attention. Then, I nodded toward the front door. One of us had to get out and find help. If I could keep Sid occupied, she might be able to escape.

"These are the ones I want," Sid announced, ripping some pages out of the binder. "Get ready to help me find them."

While he studied the papers, Addy slowly inched toward the doorway. Sid had placed the gun down on the desk, but I knew we had to be careful. Each step she took I counted as a small victory. I just hoped we'd get out of this alive.

I reached out toward the table close to me. There was a picture sitting there of my parents and me in a heavy wooden frame.

My throat felt dry. I swallowed nervously and counted to ten. Seconds later, I grabbed the frame and threw it as hard as I could at Sid, knocking the papers out of his hands. As I'd hoped, he dropped down to the ground to pick them up from the floor.

Addy ran out into the hallway, with me right behind her. I didn't look back because I could hear Sid running across the room after us. Just a few more seconds, and we'd be at the door, and freedom.

I was almost there when Sid dove for me with both hands. Addy was already at the door, turning the knob. I wiggled loose and got up.

Out of one eye, I saw Addy open the front door. Hoping to distract Sid, I turned and ran into the kitchen, hoping he would chase me and let Addy get away. It worked.

"I've got you now, Tyler!" Sid shouted.

I knew he wasn't far behind me. Desperately looking around, I grabbed the big pickle jar and hit him with it hard on the head.

He crumpled to the ground, and the jar smashed on the floor, sending glass and pickles flying everywhere. He lay moaning, holding his head.

Now it was my turn to get out of there. With the smell of pickle juice and the sounds Sid was making filling the air, I ran into the living room and through the front door. To my incredible surprise and relief, I found Jack on the front porch, standing next to Addy. Alanna was right at his side, barking and snarling.

"He's in the kitchen," I shouted.

Jack pushed Addy away and pulled out his gun. "Okay, Sid. It's all over. Come on out of there."

A few minutes later, Sid walked through the front door. He held his hands high up over his head.

CHAPTER SEVENTEEN

Later that night, things eventually calmed down. The pickle mess was even cleared up, although the smell of pickles lingered in the kitchen.

The rain and wind had transformed the whole area into a muddy mess. A few trees had been knocked down, too, but at least they hadn't hit the house or the antique shop. All in all, we'd been lucky.

"Jack said you handled yourself really well, Tyler," Grandma said. "He told me you let Addy get out of there while you led Sid into the kitchen."

"He did?"

Seeing Jack in action this afternoon on the front porch was incredible. He said he'd gone out to where Sid was staying and found Alanna tied up out back. Then, he'd rushed over here to check on things.

Grandpa reached over and put a hand on my shoulder. "You did great, Tyler. Proud of you."

That was all he said, but I'll never forget the look on his face just then.

The next morning, Addy and David's mother dropped them off at the ranch. We settled down in the living room to talk because the front porch was still drying out. My grandparents had gone into town, so we were alone.

"How's your wrist?" I asked David.

"It's better," he said. He held it up to show me how it was wrapped in a beige cloth bandage. "I'm going to try not to fall into any more mines."

"Sorry about the slingshot contest," I told him.

"So am I," he said.

Just him saying that and not blaming anyone else for his getting hurt was a big change for him. Maybe there was hope after all.

Then, I asked, "Ben, are you here?"

Ben appeared in front of us a few seconds later. "I'm glad you guys are all okay."

"I've got an idea," I said. "I don't know if it's right or not, but it might help us find your dad."

"What is it?" he asked, his eyes lighting up.

"You said you've been remembering more. I know it's hard, but I want you to remember that last day," I told him. "Where were you?"

"I was in my room, reading a book," he answered.

"Then you heard something, right?"

Ben nodded. "I ran downstairs and went outside to see what it was."

"What did you see?"

"Nothing," Ben said. "I looked to the left first because that's the direction I thought the noise came from. But there was no one there."

"What happened next?" I asked.

Ben swallowed hard. "Then I heard another noise, just like the first one. That's all I remember."

"Did the noises sound like gunshots?" I asked, holding my breath, waiting for the answer.

Ben looked down at the floor.

"Yep. They could have been," he finally said in a low voice.

"I think it was Nathan and Thomas," I told him. "They probably shot your dad first then you."

Ben's face turned pale. But he didn't say anything. It would take more prodding to find the answers that I believed were buried in his brain.

"I wondered about it when Grandpa told me that someone had set fire to the shop," I said. "That awful smell of smoke and all the damage meant no one could go in there for a long time. But I don't think someone did it because he was mad at Grandpa."

Here I stopped and looked around. Everyone was staring at me intently.

"I think the brothers did those things so no one could search the place right away. There was something they wanted to hide," I continued. "I think it's probably still in the shop. Why don't we go look for it?"

After everyone nodded, we headed out there. Inside, I went over to the corner that was furthest away from the house.

Then, working together, we moved a small table out of the way and pushed the rug back.

When I got down on my hands and knees, I saw them. There were very slight lines in the boards. They were just like the ones in the house, except these were wider.

I'd already brought out a few tools to the shop earlier in

the morning. I handed one each to Addy and David and took one myself.

After a while, we managed to pry up the large section of wood that was there. Shining the flashlight downward, I saw some rough steps, and then it looked like there was a tunnel.

I had to take a deep breath at that point because my heart started pounding. What if nothing was down there? I'd already been wrong a few times.

I started down, carefully stepping on each creaky stair. I didn't want one to break under me.

I sniffed the air and then wrinkled up my nose. Since it was shut up for so long, the air smelled weird, almost like those old newspapers, but worse.

I aimed my light at the walls and then back to the pathway. "This tunnel goes on for a ways. The brothers may have used this as a hide out before, so they knew it was here."

To the left, we saw that someone had dug out what looked to be a side passage. Then, when I flashed the light on the ground there, I saw something that made my hand shake.

There was a shallow space dug out of the earth. One of the first things we saw was a large belt buckle with a "C" in the middle. There were also bones, spread out amongst some old clothes.

"I think they surprised your dad and brought him down here," I said, looking over at Ben.

He dropped to his knees and stared at the bones. Then, he reached out to touch the belt buckle. "I guess I just needed to see for myself."

I knelt down next to him. "I'm really sorry."

"You actually found him for me. Thank you." He stretched out a hand to me.

I took it and shook it wordlessly, feeling the coolness of his skin.

Then, he turned his head to one side as if he heard something. Whatever it was, it was beyond my hearing or sight.

He turned back around and smiled one of his shy smiles. "Thank you. All of you. Now, I think it's time for me to go."

With that, he nodded and then slowly faded away, right in front of us.

Afterward, we just looked at each other. I didn't think any of us would ever be the same.

"I can't believe you really found Ben's dad," David said, staring down at the remains.

Addy was still wiping her eyes. "It's amazing."

"I think after Nathan and Thomas finished with Ben's dad, I think they must have found Ben, and shot him by the quarry," I told them. "They probably buried him and covered him with rocks, which gradually got moved one way or the other, over the years."

After that, I think we were all lost in our own thoughts for a while. I knew I'd never forget Ben. Ever.

Then, I smiled when I thought of Grandpa. I'd helped him solve his last case.

ABOUT ATMOSPHERE PRESS

Atmosphere Press is an independent, full-service publisher for excellent books in all genres and for all audiences. Learn more about what we do at atmospherepress.com.

We encourage you to check out some of Atmosphere's latest releases, which are available at Amazon.com and via order from your local bookstore:

Dancing with David, a novel by Siegfried Johnson

The Friendship Quilts, a novel by June Calender

My Significant Nobody, a novel by Stevie D. Parker

Nine Days, a novel by Judy Lannon

Shining New Testament: The Cloning of Jay Christ, a novel by Cliff Williamson

Shadows of Robyst, a novel by K. E. Maroudas

Home Within a Landscape, a novel by Alexey L. Kovalev

Motherhood, a novel by Siamak Vakili

Death, The Pharmacist, a novel by D. Ike Horst

Mystery of the Lost Years, a novel by Bobby J. Bixler

Bone Deep Bonds, a novel by B. G. Arnold

Terriers in the Jungle, a novel by Georja Umano

Into the Emerald Dream, a novel by Autumn Allen

His Name Was Ellis, a novel by Joseph Libonati

The Cup, a novel by D. P. Hardwick

The Empathy Academy, a novel by Dustin Grinnell

Tholocco's Wake, a novel by W. W. VanOverbeke

Dying to Live, a novel by Barbara Macpherson Reyelts

Looking for Lawson, a novel by Mark Kirby

ABOUT THE AUTHOR

Jan Burns has written eight nonfiction children's books and hundreds of articles and stories. She received a BA in Sociology from the University of California-Berkeley.

CPSIA information can be obtained
at www.ICGtesting.com
Printed in the USA
LVHW040508190622
721556LV00005B/158